THE CREATURE OF CRETE

with best wishes

[signature]

notreallybooks..... really good stories

The Creature of Crete

First published 2006 by notreallybooks
Reprinted 2008
Suite 111, 25 Dorset House, Chelmsford, England CM1 1TB

ISBN: 0-9552129-1-X
ISBN (13): 978-0-9552129-1-8

British Library Cataloguing in Publication Data:
A catalogue record for this book is available from the British Library

Printed in Cambridge, England, by Piggott Black Bear

John Harris would like to thank
Andrea Harris, Barbara Houseman,
Tom Morgan-Jones and Nat Scurll
for their unique and various contributions to this project,
Andrew Sheerin of dspoke.com for the brilliant website,
and Lemmy for some very wise advice a long time ago.

www.johnharristhestoryteller.com
www.notreallybooks.biz

THE CREATURE OF CRETE

STORIES FROM ANCIENT GREECE
RETOLD BY

John Harris

ILLUSTRATED BY
Tom Morgan-Jones

notreallybooks

CONTENTS

THE MONSTER KING.......
A WORD OR TWO ABOUT KING MINOS

If you look at a map of the world you will see that all around Greece there are dozens of smaller islands. You might have been to one of them on holiday, or you might know someone whose family comes from one of them. They have names like Corfu, Kephalonia, Kalymnos, and Paros, and although they are all rather different from each other they are all quite beautiful in their different ways.

These days they are part of what we call "Greece" but thousands of years ago, in the time of the Ancient Greeks, each of these islands was a separate country, a separate kingdom with its own King. Some of these kings were good men: wise, kind and brave when they had to be. They had the respect, and even the love, of the other people who lived on their island.

Some of them, however, were not so good: not so wise, brave or kind. Some were a little greedy or foolish; some could be quite cruel and mean. Some would bully their own people but be cowards in the face of danger. Some would happily put other people's lives in danger for their own greed, and many of them wanted to rule most, if not all, of the world. And perhaps the worst of them all was Minos, the king of the island of Crete. Some people called him the creature of Crete, others called him a monster, and most people agreed that when he smiled he had the cruel, lifeless eyes of a shark.

He was certainly rather full of himself. In fact the only

thing that was as big as his opinion of himself was his wealth: he was, quite probably, the richest man in the world at that time. One of the reasons he was so rich was that he found it fun to steal money from other people.

He'd wake up in the morning, have a stretch and a yawn, look around and say to himself, "I'm bored! What shall I do today?" Then a smile would flicker across his face. "I know! I'll send out a raiding party!"

And so dozens, sometimes hundreds, of his soldiers would jump into boats and sail across the sea to another island, where the people hadn't done anything to upset anyone and weren't expecting any trouble. The soldiers would charge ashore and kill anyone who got in their way. They'd find where all the treasure was kept, pile it into sacks, pile the sacks into the boats and then set off back for home.

When they got home they'd hand all the treasure over to Minos who, in turn, paid them very well. This meant, of course, that even though they knew he was a thoroughly wicked man they were loyal to him.

Minos had a wife called Pasiphae and nine children. You might think this meant he had a big happy family, but we can't be so sure of that. He didn't seem to trust them, and they certainly knew how cruel he could be. It's probably fair to say that he loved the power and wealth he got from being King more than he loved his own family. Nevertheless when something terrible happened to his youngest son, Androgeos, he took a cruel and strange revenge.

The ancient Greeks, who were very keen on sports, often held games which lasted for weeks at a time. Androgeos, a good all round athlete, had sailed over to Athens to take part in one such competition. These days Athens is the capital city of Greece but in those days it was a separate country, what was known as a city state, and the people of Athens didn't take kindly to this stranger coming from another country and winning most of the races he entered.

One night, when the games were drawing to a close, a gang of young men who'd been out drinking spotted Androgeos walking back to his lodgings.

"Hey, look!" one of them said, "there's the kid from Crete who keeps winning all the races."

"Oh, yeah," said another, "I can't stand him."

"Makes me sick!" said a third, spitting on the ground, "I had money on that last race - lost it all 'cos of him!" He spat again.

"Let's teach him a lesson," the first one suggested.

"What, like how to swim back to Crete?" One of them said and they all laughed.

"No," the first one clenched his fist tight, "I mean really teach - him - a - lesson." The others realised what he meant and started grinning. "Yeah!" They said in unison and started to follow Androgeos.

They followed him at a safe distance until they got to a deserted part of town. Androgeos, beginning to sense he was being followed, started to walk more quickly. So did the men who were following him. He had a feeling something bad was going to happen. In his hurry to get away he took a wrong turning and entered a dark and lonely alley which, to his horror, he realised had a dead end from which there was no escape.

When they were sure there was no-one watching, the Athenians followed him into the alley and set upon him with their fists and their feet. He fought back as well as he could but there were too many of them. Even after he'd

Androgeos had a bad feeling.....

been knocked to the ground they kicked him until he lay quite still and they realised he wasn't moving. Gradually they noticed the blood seeping from under his body and then, realising what they'd done, they ran away, leaving someone else to discover the body in the morning.

When Minos heard what had happened he was beyond angry, he was furious. Understandably, he felt there was something wrong with Athens if a gang of thugs could kill someone in cold blood and apparently get away with it. What was less understandable, perhaps, was that he held every single Athenian responsible - every man, woman and child - and decided they would all have to be punished. He declared war on Athens.

His soldiers attacked so swiftly and fiercely that within hours Aegeus, the King of Athens, had no choice but to surrender and begged Minos to leave his city and his people in peace.

Minos agreed on one condition: when his soldiers left for home they would take with them twentyfour children from Athens: twelve boys and twelve girls. And every year from then on the people of Athens would have to mark their defeat by sending another twelve boys and twelve girls to Crete. This puzzled Aegeus, but Minos wouldn't explain why. Those were the terms and Aegeus had to accept them. He knew he had no choice. If he didn't send the children every year from then on Minos and his soldiers would be back and all of Athens, the city and its people, would be destroyed.

A lottery was organised, but not the kind of lottery anyone wants to win. The names of all the children of the city were placed in two barrels, one for boys and one for girls, and twelve names were taken from each. When soldiers came to collect those whose names had been chosen they often had to drag them away from their parents, who wept and wailed as they were taken away. Friends and neighbours would comfort the parents while silently thanking the gods that their own children hadn't been chosen. At least not this time.

The children were loaded onto boats which set off immediately for Crete. They tried to be brave as they looked back and saw their homeland shrinking in the distance. They tried to imagine themselves as servants at Minos's castle. It couldn't be that bad a life, could it?

But they weren't going to be servants.

When they got to Crete they were taken to the castle and led down stone steps to a dark, damp dungeon. There was straw on the floor for them to sleep on but no blankets and no windows and the door was locked and bolted. Once the guards had gone away there was a strange, uncomfortable silence. No-one knew what was happening; no-one knew what to do.

But then they were given a really good meal, which made them feel a little better. The next day they were given four big meals. In fact every day they were given four or five really good meals, but no work to do and no exercise. They couldn't understand what was happening. They were locked away in a dungeon with no light, no work to do, no exercise, no idea what was happening to them or why they were there, and yet they were being well fed. And you know what happens when you eat lots and don't do any exercise: you put on weight, which is what they all did.

No-one dared ask 'Are we there yet?

And then another puzzling thing happened: One of the boys was taken away by the guards one morning, and he wasn't brought back. Not later that day, not ever. None of the guards would tell the others why he was taken away, where he was, or if he would ever be back. Then a couple of weeks later one of the girls was taken away and she too was never seen again.

This became quite a regular occurrence. Once a fortnight or so one of them would be taken out of the dungeon and that was the last the others would ever see of them. Those who were left behind wondered what had happened to their friends. Perhaps you had to be a certain weight before you could do the jobs they'd been brought to Crete to do, someone suggested, and that was why they were being so well fed. No-one knew for sure until it was their turn, but they began to realise that sooner or later their turn would surely come.

And when it was their turn they were taken along the corridors in the basement of the castle to another big, dark room which was full of rank smells of animal waste and rotting meat. Gradually, as their eyes adjusted to the darkness, they could see that in the middle of this room was a large cage. Before they realised what was happening the guard would unlock the cage door and the child would be pushed in.

The sound of the door slamming shut echoed around the room and drowned the sound of the guard running away. When the guard was gone there would be silence.

For a moment.

And then the poor child would realise there was something else already in the cage: the real creature of Crete. The child was not alone. But the creature soon would be.

THE FIRST BOY TO FLY
THE STORY OF DAEDALUS AND ICARUS

One morning, some years after the death of Androgeos and the war that followed, Minos was sitting in his State room, the room he used for meetings and big decisions. There was a huge comfortable throne for him to sit on while he held court, and a beautiful olive wood desk for him to sit at whilst writing out orders and decrees and studying maps and charts. There were rugs from all over the world on the floor and cushions which people he quite liked were allowed to sit on - those he didn't like had to stand. It was an impressive room. Anyone walking into it would realise immediately that this was a room where important decisions were made by a great and powerful King.

But Minos wasn't happy with it. In fact, he wasn't happy with any part of his castle. His private rooms, the grounds, the kitchens, the dining hall, all seemed a little....... dull. Small. Ordinary. Not quite what he wanted, not quite what he deserved. He sat on his throne and yawned loudly. Then he thought "I'm bored with this castle! It's not big enough for me, and it's not good enough either. Any fool can live in a castle - I deserve something better! After all, I am the richest and most powerful person in the world so I ought to have the most wonderful home in the world." Then he realised what he wanted: a Palace. And not just any old palace - the finest palace in the world. And he knew just who he wanted to design and build this palace.

He yelled for his Chamberlain, who arrived a moment later rather nervously.

"Good morning, your Royal Highness!" The Chamberlain trembled slightly. It was unusual to be called to the King's State Room so early and he knew it meant trouble. He just hoped it didn't mean trouble for him.

"Get me Daedalus!" Minos barked.

"Very good, your Highness," said the Chamberlain. He turned to leave, but then paused, "But your Highness, Daedalus lives a long way away."

"Then you'd better get a move on!" the King shouted.

The Chamberlain left very quickly.

Daedalus was a very clever man: architect, artist, engineer, designer, inventor, builder, draughtsman, scientist, mathematician; in fact an all round very clever chap. You name it, Daedalus could do it. His very name meant "ingenious", and it seemed there wasn't anything he couldn't put his mind to. After working all day on his designs and ideas, he'd often spend the evening relaxing by creating the most difficult puzzles you could ever imagine which no-one else could possibly do. He'd try them out on his friends and when they'd all tried and tried and eventually given up saying it was impossible, he'd show them how to do it. And once he'd shown them how, it always seemed so simple.

Daedalus didn't really want to work for Minos. Everyone had heard how unpleasant he was; however, when half a dozen of Minos' big bad soldiers kicked his front door in announcing that "Minos wants you to work for him!" he didn't feel he had much choice.

So a few days later he found himself waiting in the State Room. The soldiers who'd brought him in told him to make

when he smiled he had the
cruel, lifeless eyes of a shark

himself comfortable until the King arrived, but that was easier said than done. The fact that there were armed guards standing by each of the doors made him uncomfortable, to say the least.

He stood looking out of one of the windows at the clear blue sea, watching the sun glinting on the waves. He watched a fisherman's boat for a minute and then marvelled at how a flock of birds seemed to appear from nowhere as the fisherman pulled in his net and the birds tried to steal the fish he'd caught.

He loved the sea, and it usually left him feeling calm and relaxed, but not this morning. He realised he wasn't just nervous about meeting Minos, and it wasn't just the presence of the guards. There was something else in the room that was making him uncomfortable. He looked around and then realised what it was: as well as the man made rugs and carpets from all over the world the floor was strewn with the skins of exotic, but now very dead, animals. Some of these animal skins still had the heads on, and the eyes seemed to be staring at Daedalus. He wondered if this might be some kind of omen, a warning from the gods.

"Ah! Daedalus!" Minos's booming voice made him jump as the King burst into the room. "How nice to finally meet you! Pleasant journey?"

"I was taken from my own house and brought here against my will." Daedalus said quietly but firmly. He was a little surprised by his own courage.

"I'm so sorry," said the King as he settled himself down. "I'm afraid my boys do get a little over enthusiastic sometimes!"

"I was chained to the floor of the boat! said Daedalus.

One of the guards spoke up. "The seas can be a bit choppy this time of year, Sir," he said to Minos. "We didn't want him falling overboard or anything!"

"There you are!" said Minos, as if this was a satisfactory explanation.

"Why have I been brought here?" asked Daedalus.

"I have a job for you!" said Minos

"I'm very busy at the moment," Daedalus replied, and as soon as he saw the expression on Minos's face he knew he'd made a mistake.

"How busy?" asked the King in a rather menacing tone. Daedalus remembered that everyone else in the room had a sword at their waist.

"Well.... perhaps not hugely busy." Daedalus smiled weakly. "Why? What did you have in mind?"

"I want you to build me a palace," said the King.

"What kind of palace?"

"The finest in the world!"

"With respect," Daedalus said politely, "there must be perfectly good builders on Crete. Why me?"

"I want this done properly. There are, how shall I put it? One or two, er, special instructions."

"Such as?"

Minos pointed to a window. "You see those rocks over there, just on the edge of the island? I want it built on those rocks. Can you do that?"

"I can't see why not," Daedalus said, "but why do you want it there?"

"Because I want it to be almost like a little island all on its own. I want it to be able to withstand any kind of siege or attack."

"I see."

Minos continued with his instructions. "Amongst the rocks themselves I want you to build me boat houses so that my navy can launch an attack in any direction."

"Shouldn't be a problem."

"I haven't finished yet, listen. I want this palace to include the finest accommodation for myself and my family, excellent accommodation for my advisers, and very good accommodation for my soldiers, my sailors and my servants. We need land to tend animals on, land to grow food on, and land to train my troops on. All contained within the walls of the palace. Can you do all that?"

"Might take a little longer but I don't see why not," Daedalus said.

"Good! And one more thing...." The King looked around him at the guards at the edge of the room. He clicked his fingers and then waved his hand as a sign for them to leave. Even though the room was empty a moment later Minos lowered his voice and leaned closer towards Daedalus. "I hear you're good at creating puzzles, is that right?" he asked.

"It's a sort of hobby of mine," said Daedalus.

"Good," said the King. "Listen: down amongst the rocks themselves, among the very foundations of the building, I want you personally - " he jabbed his finger towards Daedalus to emphasise the point, "to design and build the most complicated maze in the world. I want it so complicated that although there will be a way out, no-one will ever be able to find it. Once they're in it, they're in it for good."

This was a strange request, even from a man like Minos. Daedalus was about to ask a question when the king held up a hand to stop him. "You, and you alone, will design and build it. I don't want anyone else to know about it until you've finished, and even then no-one must ever see the plans. Do you understand?"

"Well, yes, but -"

I want it built on those rocks...

"Can you do it?"

"Well, yes, I can keep the plans in my head if you want me to, but - in the basement?" he asked.

"In the basement," Minos repeated.

"Forgive me for saying so but, isn't this all a bit.... strange?" Daedalus asked. Minos gave him a cold stare but he carried on. "I mean the whole point of a maze is that you go in, and you get a bit lost, but actually it's not as bad as you think, so eventually you work out how to get out of it and it's all a bit of fun. But you do get out again. That's the point."

"Not with this one," Minos said.

"Well where's the fun in that?"

"This isn't for fun."

"Then what is it for?"

"Mind your own business," said the King. "If you want the job it's yours, and I'll pay you as much as you want," he said. "But you do exactly as I say, and you don't ask questions. Understood?"

Daedalus nodded. He had a really bad feeling about this. He knew he was in a difficult situation. He didn't like the idea of building something without knowing what it was for, but he didn't want to get on the wrong side of Minos. He was a long way from home and with Minos as an enemy he wouldn't even be safe there.

Daedalus thought about some of the awful stories he'd heard about this man. He knew that if he said no it would be very easy for the King to kill him right there and then, and no-one would ever know what happened to Daedalus. On the other hand, if he said yes he would be paid as much as he wanted. He would be rich, and he'd be able to go home feeling safer. His mind was made up. He shrugged his shoulders and said to Minos "You're paying."

"I'm glad you understand," Minos smiled. "When can you start?"

And so a ship was sent to collect all the bricklayers, plumbers, masons, carpenters and labourers who worked for Daedalus, along with his son, Icarus, who was also his assistant. As soon as they arrived on Crete they set about designing and building the finest, most beautiful, luxurious palace in the whole world.

On one of the higher levels there was a floor of private rooms for Minos. A sitting room that was bigger than most people's houses. A huge bedroom with a door leading to a bathroom which had a bath as big as most people's bedrooms. On the other side of the bedroom was a door that led to a private courtyard. Here there were lemon trees in terracotta urns so that at night, if the King couldn't sleep, all he had to do was open the doors and the scent of lemons would waft in on the night air and help him to relax.

There were meeting rooms, ceremonial rooms, offices, kitchens, servants' quarters, garrisons for the soldiers and sailors, armouries to make and store weapons, a treasury for Minos's wealth, vegetable gardens, a small farm, private gardens for Minos and his family, stables, dungeons, and even a little harbour with boat houses. There was everything Minos had asked for, but there were things he hadn't even dreamed of. Deadalus had built more than a palace: this was a self contained city by the sea.

And deep, deep, down underground, among the foundations of the palace, Daedalus had designed and built a maze that no-one would ever be able to get out of, and of which he was really rather proud. He thought it was probably the cleverest thing he'd ever designed. Once he'd

The finest palace in the whole world

started work on it he became so absorbed by what he was doing that all the doubts he'd had about the job when he was first asked simply disappeared. When it was finished he called his wonderful maze the Labyrinth.

There were two entrances, and anyone entering the Labyrinth, from either entrance, would very quickly have no idea how they'd got in, let alone how to get out. One of the entrances began as a passage leading from the dungeons, which twisted and turned until it became the Labyrinth itself. The other was carved into the rock at the harbour at the bottom of the palace, and made to look like an entrance that would lead into the Palace. The idea was that any invaders who got into the harbour would be led straight into the Labyrinth and never be seen again. When Daedalus told Minos about this the King was so delighted with the idea he roared with laughter and gripped him in a bear hug. Minos was delighted with the palace and delighted with Daedalus. Daedalus was pleased that his work was so appreciated, and delighted to be such a favourite of the king.

But his delight very quickly turned to horror when he finally realised what the Labyrinth was to be used for.

You see, Minos had a sort of pet. And we're not talking bunny rabbits or guinea pigs here. This was a huge and hideous monster about eight feet tall, a creature unlike anything else in the world. The bottom half was rather like a man but the top half was more like a bull, with two big, sharp and very nasty horns on the top of its head, strong jaws and sharp teeth. Anything that moved it would rip to shreds and eat. It liked its food fresh, juicy, warm and crunchy; and its favourite food of all was human being. This creature was called the Minotaur.

The Minotaur had been kept in a cage down in the basement of the castle, close by the dungeons. Minos was always worried that sooner or later the Minotaur, which was very strong but not exactly clever, would nevertheless realise that it probably had the strength to gradually bend the bars of the cage and eventually get free, and that would mean big trouble.

That was why he'd thought of asking Daedalus to design the Labyrinth - once the Minotaur was in there it would be safely out of harm's way.

So one night, just before everybody moved into the wonderful new palace, the small group of soldiers whose job it was to secretly feed and guard the creature mixed a powerful sleeping potion into its food. When it was safely asleep, they crept into the cage to tie it up, and in the middle of the night, under the cover of darkness, the Minotaur was carried from the castle into the new palace and down into the corridors by the dungeons. The soldiers untied the creature and then turned to leave before it woke up. Almost immediately they realised, of course, that they couldn't find their way out. They split up to explore different corridors, and never saw each other again.

Although it would never be able to find its way out, the Minotaur could hear the slightest movement and smell the slightest scent, so when it woke up that first morning in its new home it found fresh, live food wandering along the corridors of the Labyrinth.

Such was the reward with which Minos repaid the loyalty of his servants.

Anyone who upset the King in any serious way would be ordered into the Labyrinth, and sooner or later the Minotaur would find them.

we're not talking bunny
rabbits or guinea pigs here

But the creature's staple diet came in smaller packages at more regular intervals. Once a fortnight, in fact. Just as one of the children had been taken away every couple of weeks from the old castle dungeons, now they were led out of the new palace dungeon and told to walk along a particular corridor until they got to the end. They'd walk until they came to a dead end, at which they'd turn round and try to retrace their steps, only to find another dead end. Then another. And then another.

Gradually they realised they were lost, and stuck down there.

When human beings are frightened they give off a scent that other animals can pick up. The Minotaur would hear the footsteps of the lost child and follow them along the dark damp corridors, trusting its nose as much as its ears to lead it towards the poor creature. As the Minotaur drew closer the scent of fear grew stronger and clearer in its nostrils.

Some children cried for help. Others simply cried. The lucky ones didn't even see what was coming.

For all of them, there was no way out.

When Daedalus realised that this was what his great invention was actually being used for he was horrified. He'd gone to all that trouble to invent something he thought was really clever and it was being used as a home for a savage beast that ate young children! He felt awful, and he felt guilty. He remembered how uncomfortable he'd felt about taking on the job, and how he'd been too afraid to say no, even though he knew he should have done. Now he felt worse because he realised he was part of the awful fate those poor children were to meet. He felt he was, at least partly, responsible for their deaths.

But it was too late now. He'd built the Labyrinth and he couldn't take it apart. He couldn't undo what he'd done. But what he could do, he realised, was go home and warn other people about what Minos was up to, and tell them the secret of how to get out of the Labyrinth.

So the next morning he went to see Minos and presented him with the final bill for all the work that had been done on the palace.

Minos unrolled the scroll with all the accounts set out and when he got to the final total at the bottom of the scroll said, "Yes, that's fine. In fact I'll pay you twice as much as that because you've done such a good job. I'm delighted with this palace - I love it!"

"Thank you very much, your Royal Highness," said Daedalus. "I'm delighted that you're so pleased with the palace, and with that news I think my work here is done and so, with your permission, my workers and I will be leaving for home shortly."

"Your workers can leave immediately," Minos said. "My boats will take them home and they'll all be paid before they leave, but I'm afraid you and Icarus will have to stay here a little longer."

"Why" asked Daedalus. "Is there a problem?"

"Well yes, in a way." the King began.

"But you've just said everything's fine," Daedalus protested.

"Oh there's no problem with the building itself," Minos began to explain, "no, no, no, the building's wonderful. It's just that, well er, how can I put this?" He paused for a moment. "You know the secret of the Labyrinth, don't you, Daedalus?" he asked.

"Well of course I do," said Daedalus. "I designed and built it myself, just like you asked me to. I know how to get out of it, but no-one else does."

"Ah, yes, you see..... there's my problem," said the King. "I simply can't allow that secret to leave this island."

"Well I'm not going to tell anyone."

"How can I be sure of that?" the King asked.

"I give you my word!"

"And how do I know that you're going to keep your word?"

"I promise I will!" Daedalus shrugged his shoulders.

"And how do I know that you're going to keep your promise?" Minos asked.

"Er.... I promise to er... keep my promise."

"And how do I know that you're going to keep that promise?" the king asked. Daedalus knew Minos was making fun of him.

"Well, I, er... promise that I'll keep my promise to keep my promise," Daedalus said, and he knew as he spoke how ridiculous it sounded.

"This isn't really getting us anywhere, is it?" asked Minos. Daedalus shook his head. "You see my problem?" Minos continued, "It's nothing personal, but I can't trust you. I don't trust anyone. I haven't survived this long by trusting people. I'm afraid there's no choice: you and Icarus will have to stay here a little longer."

"How long exactly?" Daedalus asked.

"Ah well, that depends, doesn't it?"

"On what?"

"On how long you live!" Minos seemed to find this rather amusing and had a little chuckle about it. Daedalus didn't think it was at all funny.

Minos went on to explain. "When you die you won't be able to tell anyone the secret of the Labyrinth, so that's when Icarus will be able to take you home. You know what they say: dead men tell no tales!"

"So you're keeping me prisoner on this island?"

"No, no - no - no - no - no! You're my honoured guests! You and your son can have your very own suite of rooms on the top floor of the palace. The finest of everything will be yours for the asking - food, clothes, wine, furnishings, entertainment - you name it, you can have it - apart from a boat, that is." He chuckled again at this.

"So we're prisoners, under house arrest," said Daedalus.

"Absolutely not! You have the freedom of my Kingdom." Minos held his arms out wide as if to emphasise the point. "You can go anywhere you like on Crete at any time." He paused for a second, and then added "As long as you don't mind one of my soldiers being with you, of course."

"What if we try to escape?" Daedalus asked.

"They've already been told to cut you into little pieces," he smiled.

"Well it sounds to me as though we're prisoners!"

"It depends on how you look at it," Minos explained. "I'm giving you a choice: You and Icarus can have a suite of rooms at the top of my wonderful palace, the finest of everything whenever you ask, the freedom to go anywhere on my island, or...." he raised a finger threateningly, "If you don't want the rooms at the top then you can go down to the very bottom and see if you can work your way out of the Labyrinth before you know what catches up with you." He paused for a moment and then asked "So, which is it to be?" Daedalus knew he had no choice.

"I'll take the rooms," he said.

"Yes, I rather thought you might," said Minos. "Welcome to Crete - enjoy your stay!"

And so Daedalus and Icarus moved into rooms at the top of the palace. Daedalus was very unhappy. He knew he was a prisoner, even if it was in a very comfortable prison, and he knew that in many ways it was his own fault. He was just as angry with himself for getting into this mess as he was with Minos for putting him there.

Icarus, on the other hand, was delighted. He was living like a prince. He had a luxurious home, with plenty to eat and drink; he quickly made friends with the other young people who lived and worked at the palace; and it seemed as if every night there was a party somewhere that he was invited to.

He walked into the living room one morning to find his dad sitting quietly.

"Morning, Dad!" Icarus yawned.

"Morning, son."

"Sleep well?" he asked.

"Not really," said Daedalus.

"That's a shame. I slept like a log."

"I know. It's almost midday."

"Well, I was out late last night."

"I know. I heard you come in."

"And the beds here are so comfortable."

"Mmmmm."

"And the air's so fresh!" Icarus went over to the window and took a deep breath. "Sea air always makes me sleep well!"

"Oh I'm so glad!" Daedalus said in a rather sarcastic tone.

"What's the matter with you?" Icarus asked. Daedalus almost growled the reply. "You know full well what the matter is. I want to go home!"

"This is home," said Icarus.

Icarus couldn't understand
why his dad was so unhappy

"No it isn't!"

"Well it is now!" Icarus pointed out. "Let's face it - we're not going anywhere else!"

"And you're happy just to accept that are you?" his father asked.

"I don't see there's much we can do about it!" Icarus said. There was silence for a moment, and then he added "Anyway, I like it here!"

"Oh that's all right, then!"

"What is the matter?" he asked. "It's good here! Of course I like it - who wouldn't?"

"I don't!" his father snapped, "and I want to go home!"

"Why?" Icarus asked. "Look around you. You have to admit this is much more comfortable than our old home. This living room's about ten times the size of the one we had. We each have huge comfortable bedrooms with our own bathrooms and -"

"I know!" Daedalus almost barked. "I designed them!"

"Yes! And a very good job you did too!" Icarus tried to persuade him. "Look dad, we have everything we want here and it's all better than what we had at home! Any time of the day or night we can send down to the kitchens and get anything we want to eat or drink; the food's brilliant and the wine's better than at home."

"I would still rather be home."

"But why? If we went home now we'd have to work very hard to get enough money to buy all this, but if we stay here we get it all for free! We never have to work again! We're gentlemen of leisure! I feel like a prince!"

"And I want to go home!"

"Yes - I know - but why?" Icarus really couldn't understand.

"It's a matter of principle," Daedalus explained. "I want my freedom."

"But you've got your freedom," Icarus argued. "It's not as if we're prisoners."

"That's exactly what we are," said his father.

"No we're not! We can go anywhere we like. That's not being a prisoner, is it?"

"We can go anywhere we like - on this island," Daedalus reminded him. "And wherever we go we have armed guards with us. Anywhere we go, they go, and if we try to get away from them -" he didn't finish the sentence but made the gesture of slitting his throat instead.

"They're all right," Icarus said. "They're quite nice chaps if you take the trouble to get to know them."

"I don't want to," Daedalus was beginning to sound a bit sulky.

"They're only doing their job," Icarus continued. "They don't stick right beside you, they just need to keep an eye on you and know where you are. If I go to a taverna with my mates they always sit at another table."

"Oh, how considerate of them!"

"All right then, Dad," Icarus sighed, "let's face facts." He pointed to the door leading out to the rest of the palace. "On the other side of those doors there are two armed soldiers. Twenty-four hours a day, seven days a week. Anywhere we go, they go too. So if we're going to go home we can't just walk through the door 'cos -" and he made the same throat-slitting gesture. "So the only way out would be through the window." He went back over to the window. "But let's just have a look, shall we? Oh, dear!" he called back across the room. "We're about two hundred feet up, and there's nothing but a sheer drop down to sharp, craggy rocks which would be very nasty if we landed on them. Then, for as far as anyone can see, there's the sea itself, and not much else. We haven't got a boat. We can't swim all that way and, anyway, the sea's full of all sorts of wicked, nasty beasties, so we wouldn't get very far even if we tried," he turned to look back at Daedalus. "So unless you can find a way of flying home, dad, I suggest you get used to living here. It's really not that bad!"

And with that he finished his breakfast and went out for the rest of the day, leaving poor Daedalus feeling very alone.

Icarus thought that was the end of the matter. He thought he'd made it quite clear to his dad why there was no point in even thinking of going home, and why he didn't want to go anyway. He was perfectly happy where he was, and didn't see why his dad couldn't be as happy there as he was.

And over the next few weeks it did seem as if his dad was getting used to being there and beginning to enjoy it. Gradually he stopped moaning about it and then began to be more cheerful. In fact over the next few weeks Icarus started to see quite a change in his father. Instead of loafing around lifeless and glum, or being grumpy and snapping at everyone, Daedalus became quite happy and seemed to be excited about life again. He made the effort to be friendly to people and even made some friends of his own. And sometimes he could be annoyingly cheerful at breakfast while Icarus was still waking up from a late night out the night before.

Most significant of all, he started to work again, which Icarus knew was a good sign. One morning when Icarus had said he'd be out for the whole day he suddenly needed

Icarus was delighted that
his dad was working again

to nip home for something. He walked into the living room to find his father kneeling on the floor with all sorts of plans and sketches and pages of calculations laid out all over the living room floor.

"What's this?" Icarus asked. "Are you working on something?"

Daedalus seemed a bit flustered and blushed slightly. "Well, er, in a manner of speaking -"

"Oh good! What is it?" Icarus glanced down at the plans but his father covered them up.

"It's a secret," Daedalus said. "Something for Minos. Very hush - hush, so don't say a word please."

"Why would I?"

"No - I mean it!" His father spoke vehemently. "You're a good boy but I know what happens when you get chatting with your friends. This is really serious. If you breathe a word of it to anyone we could both be in big trouble."

"Okay."

"And don't mention it to Phaedra!" He added. Phaedra was one of Minos's daughters, and a good friend of Icarus. "If Minos hears that I've let anyone - even you - know I'm working on this he'll be furious."

"Wow!" said Icarus. "Must be really serious stuff."

"You've no idea," said his father, rather mysteriously.

"Fair enough," said Icarus, and didn't give it a second thought. He was just glad - and relieved - to think that Daedalus was finally settling down to life on Crete.

But he wasn't.

Daedalus wasn't working on something for Minos, he was working on something for himself. And he'd got the idea from something Icarus had said.

Icarus had said that unless Daedalus could find a way of flying home he'd better get used to living at the palace. Of course he hadn't meant it, he was just trying to make a point. But it gave Daedalus an idea.

All Minos's servants had been told that Daedalus could have anything he wanted, apart from weapons and a boat. So when the kitchen staff got a message asking for a sack of mixed seeds to be sent up to Daedalus's rooms they didn't bother to ask what he wanted them for, they just sent them up.

A week or so later he sent for another sack, and again no-one thought to ask why.

A couple of weeks later they sent him another sack, and a couple of weeks after that another one, and so on. No-one knew why. No-one asked why. No-one really cared. In fact this went on for nearly eighteen months and in all that time no-one had any idea what he was up to. Not even Icarus.

But then Daedalus woke him up very early one morning, even before dawn had broken.

"What is it?" Icarus yawned loudly.

"Sssshhhh...." Daedalus put his finger to his lips.

"What's going on?"

"Come into the living room, I've got something to show you."

Icarus sat up in bed and gathered his thoughts. "It's a bit early, isn't it? What time is it?" he asked as he followed him into the living room.

Again Daedalus put a finger to his lips as Icarus walked in and then pointed to the front door, on the other side of which there would be two guards even at this time in the morning. "We have to be quiet," he whispered. Then he rolled back the carpet in the living room and for the first time Icarus noticed a trap door. His father lifted it up to reveal a secret chamber he'd made for himself. He reached down into the chamber and produced two bundles of what looked like feathers strung together with fine silk.

"What are those?" Icarus whispered.

"What do they look like?"

"They look like wings, but -"

"Exactly!" said Daedalus.

"But what are they for?" Icarus asked. "And where did you get them from?"

"I made them myself."

"How?"

"I've been feeding the birds around here for over a year now, early in the morning and late at night, and taking a feather from each of them in exchange." He explained. "I've used the feathers to make these wings!"

"Oh that's nice!" Icarus yawned. "They look really pretty. Can I go back to bed now? I'm very tired!"

"No," said Daedalus. "Take your night shirt off."

"Huh?"

"Just do as I say!"

Icarus knew from the look on his dad's face that he was not in the mood to argue, so he took off his night-shirt. While he was doing this Daedalus lit some candles and then stood behind him.

"Keep perfectly still," Daedalus warned.

Icarus felt a sharp, hot pain on his shoulders. "Ow!" he yelped. "What are you doing?" Then there was another one, and then another and then another. Daedalus was pouring the hot wax from the candles all over Icarus's neck, arms, shoulders and back.

"Sssssshhhhh!" his father said.

"It hurts!"

"It'll be over in a minute."

Icarus flinched again with the pain. Before he could say anything his dad said, "Don't be such a baby!"

"Yes, but -" he started to protest.

"Honestly! You're like a big girl!"

"I am not!"

"Shush! Don't let the guards hear you!"

Icarus decided not to argue any more, it wasn't worth it. After a minute or two the pain did seem to die down as his father had said it would. Or Icarus had got used to it. "There," his dad whispered after a minute or two. "Finished. What do you think?"

Icarus couldn't see his back but he lifted his arms and was amazed to see wings unfurl all the way from his wrists right down to his waist. "Wow! That's amazing!" he said. "They fit perfectly and when I spread my arms out they open like real wings!"

"I know, I designed them!" said Daedalus. "Now I want you to do the same for me."

Daedalus took off his own night-shirt and lit some more candles. While he stood quite still Icarus stood behind him and poured the wax all over his neck and arms and back and then attached the second pair of wings, which fitted as perfectly as his own did. Daedalus turned round and smiled at Icarus.

"They're great, Dad," said Icarus, "next time we get invited to a fancy dress party we can go as a pair of eagles. I'm going back to bed now. How do you get them off?"

"No you're not," said Daedalus. "We're going home."

Now it was Icarus's turn to smile. "All right, Dad," he said. "You've had a laugh and the wings are very nice but I really do need to get more sleep."

"Stay where you are!" Daedalus commanded. Again Icarus looked at him and tried to read his face. "You're

"when I spread my arms out
they open like real wings!"

serious aren't you?" he asked.

"Yes."

"Oh, come on!" Icarus laughed. His dad's expression didn't change and Icarus began to see just how serious he was. "Have you been drinking?" Icarus asked after a moment.

"Of course not!"

"Well you can't blame me for asking - this is a ridiculous idea!"

"Think for a moment, Icarus," Daedalus spoke slowly and carefully, "when was the last time one of my ideas didn"t work?"

It was a good question, and Icarus knew the answer. "Fair enough," he said. "So far every idea you've ever had has worked brilliantly. But you know what they say: there's a first time for everything. And I have a sneaky, horrible suspicion this just might be the first time you've got it wrong. So if it's okay with you I'll go back to bed now. Night night!" He turned to go.

"Icarus!" His father spoke quietly but urgently, in a way that stopped Icarus in his tracks. He turned round and saw his father pointing across the room. "Get out onto that window ledge," he ordered.

"What???!!!!"

"As your father I command you: Window ledge. NOW!"

"Uuuuuurrrgh!" Icarus growled in protest but knew it was useless. He went over to the biggest window, opened it and climbed out onto the ledge. A moment later his father joined him. Dawn was just breaking and the light from the east was beginning to bathe that side of the palace in a warm glow. But it was still rather chilly.

"Dad, this is ridiculous!" Icarus protested. "I am standing on a window ledge about two hundred feet above the sea wearing my underpants and a pair of wings that don"t belong to me and you want me to jump home?"

"It's not quite as simple as that," said Daedalus.

"Oh that's funny! I didn't think it would be!"

"It's quite straightforward as long as you listen, so listen carefully: when you jump you need to spread your arms and then the wings will enable you to glide gently downwards"

"I don't want to go downwards," Icarus interrupted.

"Just listen!" Daedalus snapped. "I calculate that with the wind speed as it is this morning it would take you about fifteen minutes to glide down to the sea. Don't go down to the sea. You've got a good ten minutes to get the hang of using your arms like real wings to gain speed and height so that you're flying rather than gliding."

"All right, Dad, tell you what - if it's that easy why don't you go first and show me how it's done?"

"No, I want to go behind you because I know what I have to do. I've spent a year working this out, you haven't. If you get into difficulties and I'm behind you I'll be able to help, but if I'm in front of you I won't see if you're having difficulties so I won't be able to help."

"Mmmm. "Difficulties" is not the word I most want to hear when I'm standing on a window ledge before I've even had breakfast," said Icarus and he started to turn. "I think I'll just go in now -"

"Stay where you are!" His dad barked.

"Dad this is stupid!" Icarus pleaded. "We'll die! It's not going to work!"

"It'll work! I promise you it'll work! All you have to do is remember not to fly too low because if you're too close to the waves the spray will add weight to your wings and pull you down," and then he added "and don't fly too high either. Not too high and not too low. Nice, steady course."

"I don't want to do this!"

"It'll be all right, I promise!"

"But Dad -"

"We haven't got much time - if they see what we're doing they'll kill us!"

"Well excuse me for stating the obvious but if we jump we're going to die anyway!"

"We won't!"

"We will!"

"We won't! I promise!"

"Don't make promises you can't keep."

"I can keep this one."

"Really?"

"I can prove to you this will work."

"How?"

With a nifty piece of footwork Daedalus kicked Icarus on his bottom.

For a split second Icarus teetered on the edge, too shocked and frightened to say or do anything, unable to believe what his father had just done. His arms waved helplessly in the air for a second as he tried to recover his balance and get back on the ledge but it was too late, he was already leaning too far. For a second he was leaning forward off the windowledge at fortyfive degrees and then he started to fall the hundreds of feet down towards the sharp craggy rocks between the palace and the sea.

He screamed in terror and then pain as the wind caught in his feathers and yanked his arms wide apart. But then his fall seemed to slow down and then stop. For a moment he was suspended in mid-air and then a gust of wind pushed him forward and he was gliding with his wings spread wide.

Once he'd got his breath back he remembered what his father had told him to do. He moved his arms and could see immediately that it was going to work, but it was going to be hard work. Then he thought it was going to be too hard, his arms were already starting to ache. He tried moving his shoulders as well as his arms and realised this was what he had to do.

If he used his whole body, almost as if he was swimming in the air, he had complete control and it was wonderful. "Oh wow!" he called out. "It works! Dad!" he called back over his shoulder, "It works! Yippeeeee!!!!!

And when he saw that Icarus was safely away Daedalus jumped as well.

Icarus was delirious. He'd never experienced anything quite like this, and had never expected to. Once he'd got over his initial fear, and got the hang of using the muscles in his upper body to move the wings and those in his legs and lower back to keep his legs straight and help with steering, he began to realise how brilliantly Daedalus had designed the wings. They really did make it easy for him to fly, and flying was the most wonderful feeling he could ever have imagined.

He had a sense of absolute freedom, but more than that. There was something quite exhilirating about what he was doing, as if all the sports he'd ever taken part in, all the games he'd ever played, were rolled into one and he was enjoying all of them together at the same time. He felt a rush of energy, excitement and pride that he could never have felt before because he was doing something no-one else had done before: he was flying!

He couldn't contain his excitement, couldn't help but call out.

"Dad, this is fantastic!

Wheeeeeeeeeeeeeeeeeeeeeeeeeeeeeee!"

"This is fantastic! Wheeeeeeeeeeeeeeeeeeeeeeeeeeeeee!"

And once he was really confident he started to experiment. "Yeeheeeeeeeeeee!" He lowered his left arm slightly and raised his right by the same amount and began to tilt over to the left. Then he tried the other way. "Oh, wow! Watch this! Whoooo-hoooo!" he rolled right over and came back upright again. His dad called something to him but he couldn't hear what.

Then he tried twisting at the waist and found that as his body curved he went into an arc that became a full circle and for a moment he spiralled downwards until he straightened himself out again and used his arms to regain height. "Ha! See that? This is incredible!" Again Daedalus shouted something but he was too far away by now for Icarus to hear properly.

You might have thought that making all this noise was not a good idea when they were trying to sneak away, but in fact it turned out to be useful. At that time in the morning the only people who heard Icarus screaming and hollering were two of Minos's soldiers who were on the early morning shift guarding the entrance to the palace.

"Oi!" one of them called to the other and pointed at Icarus. "What's that?"

The second guard walked over to the first to get a closer look. "Big bird?" he shrugged.

"There's another!" the first guard pointed to Daedalus.

"Oh, yeah...... they're too big to be birds."

"You're right!" the first guard said, "you know what they are? They're men with feathers! They're flying!!"

"Oh, yeah! isn't that clever?"

The first guard suddenly realised there was only one person clever enough to work out how to fly. "It's Daedalus and his son! They're getting away!" He took out his sword and waved it helplessly in the air. "Oi! You two!" he called.

"Get back here now!"

"Quick!" the second guard said to him, "go and tell the King they're getting away!"

"Not a good idea," the first one shook his head.

"Why not? We're supposed to tell him if something happens."

"Yes, but think about it: we're on sentry duty, aren't we?" The other one nodded. "We're supposed to stop people getting in.... or out. And if we go and tell the King that Daedalus and what's his name have flown away he'll say we've failed in our duty as sentries." The dawn of realisation crept on the second guard's face and turned to horror as the first one continued. "We tell Minos what we've just seen and he'll send us down to the Labyrinth."

"What do we do?" Asked the second.

"We never, ever, tell a soul." They shook hands and spent the rest of the morning marching backwards and forwards in front of the Palace, but with their heads firmly down so all they could see was the ground. And they never did tell anyone what they'd seen. Which, of course, gave Daedalus and Icarus all the time they needed to fly away.

By now Icarus was some way ahead of his father and he was amazed at how much he could see. The sun was climbing into the sky and there were just a few clouds quite a long way off to his right. Below him the water was so clear that he could see the darker rocky patches where the sea was shallower. Over to his left he could make out a small fishing boat with a school of dolphins leaping in and out of the water on either side of it. In front of him, but a considerable way off, was the island they were flying towards. "Come on, dad!" he called over his shoulder, "you're too slow!"

"Be careful!" Daedalus called to him, but he doubted Icarus could hear.

"Look!" cried Icarus. "I can go as fast as these birds, and just as high!"

"Careful!" This time the wind seemed to carry the warning.

"I'm all right!" Icarus called back.

But then he would say that, wouldn't he? Most young men have a tendency to show off a little, and Icarus was no different from the others.

"Whooo-hooo! Get out of my way, seagull!"

Icarus could hear his father shouting something, but at this height and distance it was hard to make out what it was. It sounded like "Dough die doo die". Below him Icarus noticed a shoal of fish suddenly scatter in all directions as a bigger creature, one whose shape he didn't recognise, seemed to appear from nowhere. It swallowed some of the fish and then disappeared just as suddenly and he realised it had gone back down, deeper beneath the waves.

"Dow die doo die!" Daedalus shouted again.

"What?" Icarus looked back over his shoulder but couldn't even see his father.

"Dow - die - doo - die!" His father sounded quite agitated, but Icarus still couldn't work out what he meant.

"Save your breath, Dad! We'll be home in no time at this rate!" Icarus shouted. "Look!" He called a moment later. "I'm really getting the hang of this!" Spreading his wings as wide as he could and arching his back he let the wind catch him and flip him right over three hundred and sixty degrees so that a moment later he was back again facing the same way. "Whoo - hooo!" he called, "did you see that?"

"Dow - die - doo - die!" the cry came again.

Then Icarus saw an eagle approaching from his left. It looked as majestic and graceful as it would have done from the ground, but now Icarus had a better understanding of how much work was involved in appearing so graceful. He remembered his father telling him when he was a little boy that the eagle could fly higher than any other creature in the world. "He he! Not any more," he said to himself as he flew higher and circled round the eagle.

The eagle looked at Icarus and then flew away and upwards.

"You want a contest? Fine!" Icarus said and flew higher than the eagle.

The eagle screeched rather aggressively and flew higher than Icarus.

So Icarus flew higher than the eagle.

So the eagle flew higher than Icarus.

Again Icarus pushed himself higher than the eagle. To gain height meant he had to push his arms straight forward and then arc them back behind him, but it was more like pulling and pushing on branches to climb quickly up a tree than the gentle, flowing movement of swimming. It was very hard work on the shoulders and the arms, and he was developing an ache across his shoulders and down his back, but he was determined to at least match the eagle.

Eventually Icarus was so high that the eagle either couldn't, or wouldn't, fly any higher. With another loud screech the eagle peeled off and flew away, downwards, leaving Icarus alone in the sky, flying higher than any other creature had ever flown before.

He looked down at everything below him: land, sea, fish, boats, even the clouds seemed to be lower than he was. In fact the only thing that he was certain was still higher than him by now was the sun, beaming down on everything, splashing the sea with patches of silver and gold mixed in with the blue.

Then something seemed to flash past him out of the corner of his eye. What was that? he wondered. He wasn't even sure he'd actually seen something or just imagined it.

A moment later there was another one on the other side. Small, shiny. Too small to be a bird, and too quick, and when he looked round he couldn't see anything. It must have been a trick of the light.

"Dow - die - doo - die!" Daedalus sounded faint and far away. Icarus had almost forgotten about his father and he was so much higher and further away by now there was no chance of actually being able to hear what he was shouting. He felt a little irritated that Daedalus was still giving out orders when he was obviously doing so well. Why can't he leave me to get on with it? he wondered. Again, out of the corner of his eye, he saw something flash past. Perhaps that's what dad was trying to tell me about, he thought, but he couldn't understand why. Then there was another. And another and another and another in quick succession, and then he actually caught a brief glimpse of one. With a shock of horror he realised what they were, and in that same awful split second he realised what it was his dad was shouting. His dad was shouting the same instructions he'd given him when they were standing together on the window ledge: "Dow - die - doo - die!" Was "Don't - fly - too - high!"

But that's what he was doing. He was flying too high, too close to the sun, and what he could see flitting past out of the corners of his eyes were the first few feathers beginning to come loose as the warmth of the sun started to melt the wax that was holding the wings in place.

Before he could do anything about it there was a sudden "Sllluuurrrppp!" sound as one whole wing peeled off and disintegrated into a million feathers that started to flutter down towards the sea.

Icarus followed seconds later.

Daedalus was helpless. He'd known for some time what was going to happen but now he could do nothing but watch as his son tumbled down, down, down through the sky, feathers and bits of broken wing spinning off in all directions, and when he hit the sea it was with so much force it might as well have been a stone wall.

All that could be seen of Icarus now was a pool of wax on the waves, and a flurry of feathers still fluttering down towards the sea. As Daedalus flew over the spot where Icarus had fallen in, the beautiful clear blue sea turned, for a moment, bright red as one of the beasts that lived under the water bit into Icarus.

And that was the end of the first boy to fly.

If there's a moral to this story, (something you can learn or think about) perhaps it's this:

The next time an adult says to you "I wouldn't do that if I were you." It might not be because they're boring old fogeys who want to spoil your fun. It could be because they've got an older, wiser, head on their shoulders and they can see more of the dangers ahead than you can.

Then again, it could be because they really are that boring and they really do want to spoil your fun after all.

But before you choose to ignore advice in future, stop and think for a moment, and remember what happened to the boy who flew too high.

Ooops...

THE HERO WHO WAS ALSO A COWARD
THE STORY OF THESEUS, ARIADNE, AND A LITTLE UNPLEASANTNESS

King Aegeus had a problem. A problem which, as you know, cropped up once a year when he had to arrange a lottery to find the names of twelve children who were to be sent from Athens to King Minos at Crete.

Until now the people of Athens had assumed - or perhaps hoped would be a better way of putting it - that the children were taken to be servants in Minos' palace. Their heartbroken parents consoled each other with talk of the new life their children were living, in which they were safe and happy.

But gradually, over the years, rumours of what really happened to the children began to reach Athens. Stories began to circulate of children being taken to a part of the palace and never being seen again. As always happens with sketchy stories and rumours, the missing parts of the stories began to be filled in by those who told them. Some people had heard of parts of the Palace that were under strict guard at all times because Minos didn't want anyone to know what was there. Other stories told of strange noises seeming to come from under the very Palace itself - growls and howls, screams and cries. Gradually these stories seemed to merge together and - unusually for rumours - more or less hit on the truth.

But even when the Athenians had realised what was happening to their children Aegeus seemed unable or unwilling to do anything about it, and his people started to get angry.

Outside Aegeus's castle a crowd had gathered demanding that the King put a stop to the lottery. He tried to reason with them, but they wouldn't listen. He reminded them that if the children weren't sent to Crete Minos's soldiers would be back in no time at all; the whole city would be destroyed and everyone in it, including them, killed. But they wouldn't listen. They'd had enough and they wanted change.

Aegeus himself had a son, a young man named Theseus. He was tall, strong, brave, at times a little hot-headed and tempestuous. Aegeus admired his son's spirit but worried that he was too quick tempered to be a wise and good King.

"Father! What's going on?" Theseus asked as he stormed into the throne room. "There's a crowd outside looking very angry."

"Oh hello, Theseus," the King said. "They are angry. It's the lottery - "

"I know what they're protesting about," his son interrupted. "But why are you holding it?"

"I have no choice. You know that."

"But when you first agreed to Minos's demands everyone thought the children were to work as servants."

"Well, yes..."

"But now we know what really happens to them!"

"We don't," his father pointed out. "What we've heard are only rumours and I can't react just to rumours. I need proof." There was a slight pause and then he added "It doesn't make any difference anyway. If we go back on the deal you know what will happen: Minos will send his army over here and there'll be a full scale war and if that happens believe me: we will lose."

"But we can't just sit here and do nothing!" Theseus argued.

"What choice do I have, son?" his father asked. "Do I send a small number of children to Crete every year, knowing they will probably die? Or do I go back on the agreement I reached with Minos and bring about a war in which probably all my people - including those who are protesting outside at the moment - will die?"

"You don't have to do either," Theseus said.

"What do you mean?"

"Cancel the lottery. I'll go instead."

"What?" the King was horrified. "But then I'll lose you!"

"You won't lose me. I'll talk to Minos. He'll see sense."

"He won't listen to you. He doesn't listen to reason."

"I'll make him!"

"You're more likely to end up fed to some sort of monster yourself."

"Fine. If all the rumours turn out to be true then I'll get the chance to do something about it and then all this will be over!"

There was a moment's pause while Aegeus thought about it. Then he took a deep breath and said, "No."

"No what?" asked Theseus.

"You can't go," said his father.

"I'm your best chance," Theseus said.

"You're my only son."

"And you don't want to lose me."

"Precisely."

"Then you have to imagine how the parents of all those children who've gone before must feel. How can you let this carry on?"

Aegeus thought long and hard while Theseus sat and stared at him. Eventually he sighed and said softly, "I can't let you go." Theseus slammed the palms of his hands on his thighs and then held out his arms in a gesture of frustration, but Aegeus continued. "It's for the good of the country. If I lose you who will become King when I die? It's a question of stability."

"That's just an excuse!" Theseus said.

"You can't go," said his father. "I forbid it."

"You can't let those children go! I forbid that!" his voice suddenly boomed and he seemed to fill the room. "I'm going to Crete and I'll sort this out for once and for all!"

Aegeus could see Theseus's mind was set. He was worried that he would lose his son but he was also proud. Proud of the strength of his son's feelings, his bravery and determination. He even admired the way in which his own son was standing up to him. He realised he had no choice. He had to let Theseus go because he'd go anyway. "Promise me you'll be careful," he sighed. Theseus smiled when he said this.

"I'll be as careful as I can be."

"I'll worry about you!" he took one of Theseus' hands in his own.

"I know," Theseus held his father's hand with both of his.

"Then do something for me," Aegeus asked.

"What?"

"Take a set of white sails as well as the usual black ones. If you succeed in your task then on your way back hoist the white sails as a sign that you're coming home safely. Word will reach me before you get back and at least that way I'll know as soon as I can, one way or the other."

"All right," Theseus smiled. "I'll take a set of white sails if it'll keep you happy."

Theseus very quickly gathered together a group of brave soldiers and sailors. Once word got out about his plan there was no shortage of volunteers, despite the dangers involved in the mission. Within a few days they set sail for Crete.

Minos's spies must have heard they were on their way, because as soon as they approached his island they were met by some of Minos's own ships and brought into port at Crete. And then they were brought to the palace to meet Minos himself.

They were left waiting in Minos's state room for what seemed like a deliberately rude length of time. They were given comfortable cushions to sit on, but armed guards made certain they wouldn't be able to leave the room. Eventually he arrived.

"Gentlemen! Welcome!" His voice boomed as he swept in, followed by an entourage of courtiers, but Theseus could see through the smile on his face. Theseus's crew stood and bowed politely. "I'm so sorry I've kept you here for so long," said Minos, "matters of state, you understand. I trust you've been comfortable." Some of them nodded and mumbled. "Excellent!" he grinned, "please - be seated!" And as they sat down again he asked "And which one of you is the young Prince Theseus?"

"I am." Theseus bowed before Minos.

"Theseus! I'm honoured to meet you!" Minos shook his hand and then signalled for someone to step forward. "This is my daughter Ariadne." As Ariadne stepped forward Theseus was immediately struck by the differences between Minos and his daughter. Where his eyes had a shark like,

She held his hand a fraction
longer than was necessary

dead quality, hers were deep brown but sparkling and alive. Where his smile was fake and meant to be slightly threatening, hers was genuine and warm. Her eyes looked deep into Theseus's as she held out her hand.

"How do you do?" she asked.

"How do you do?" Theseus replied. There was a moment's pause in which Theseus felt that she held his hand a fraction longer than was necessary, but then her father's voice boomed out and the mood was broken.

"And tell me, how is your father these days?" Minos asked.

"He is well, thank you, sir."

"Good, good!" Minos beckoned Theseus to sit down beside him as Ariadne seemed to retreat into the background. "And to what do we owe the honour of this visit?" He asked.

"I have come to discuss the terms of the arrangement you made with my father." Theseus tried to appear cool as he said this but his heart was thumping.

"Really?" Minos raised his eyebrows. "In what way.... "discuss" exactly?"

"We know what happens to the children we send you every year." Theseus began to explain.

"Go on..."

"And now that we know what happens we're not prepared to send you any more."

"Really?" Minos stared into Theseus's eyes for what seemed like an awfully long time. Eventually he asked, "Are you absolutely sure about this?"

"Absolutely." Theseus said firmly. There was another pause.

"Well, that's your decision," Minos sighed, "but you do realise what the consequences of that decision will be, don't you?"

"That's what I'm here to discuss."

All pretence at friendliness suddenly disappeared from Minos's face. "I see no need to discuss this," he snarled.

"I do," said Theseus.

"If your father does not send me the children that should be here within the next few days he knows what will happen: I will launch an attack on Athens and my soldiers will not rest until there is nothing left of your father's kingdom. Nothing at all. No buildings, no people. No crops, trees, plants or animals. Absolutely nothing. Do I make myself clear?" Minos asked.

"The children are not coming," Theseus said. "I'm here in their place."

"Really?"

"Really."

"There are no more boats following you from Athens with a new load of children on board?"

"No."

"In that case, Theseus, you're no longer my guest. You're my hostage. Remove his weapons and take him away!" Minos ordered his guards. They grabbed Theseus, whose crew immediately leapt to their feet. "Sit down immediately or you'll be taken away with him!" Minos barked. They looked towards Theseus, who nodded for them to sit back down again. "You can sail back to Athens if you want to," Minos told them, "or you can wait for him. But he will only be released when the next lot of children arrive."

"They won't arrive!" Theseus repeated.

"Then you have two weeks," said Minos. "If they're not here by then you go into the Labyrinth." Then he turned to the crew and said, "You may go now."

The Captain looked to Theseus, who nodded. As they

walked past Theseus on the way out the Captain whispered, "In two weeks we can get back to Athens and be back again with reinforcements."

"No," said Theseus. "Wait in the harbour for me."

"I don't understand."

"Wait for me - there's something I need to do, but as soon as I've done it I'll be with you. Don't leave without me."

"Aye aye, sir," said the Captain and he and the crew were gone. As the sound of their footsteps on the stone corridors died away Minos turned to Theseus.

"Well now, young Prince. You are suddenly so very alone."

"That doesn't bother me."

"I'll give you one last chance. Go home now and persuade your father to change his mind. He'll change it sooner or later. It'd be a shame for him to have to lose a son before he sees sense. Believe me, I know how hard it is to lose a son."

"He won't lose a son. You'll lose a monster."

"Ha! Ha!" this time the laughter seemed genuine. "I like your confidence. Let's see if you feel as confident in a day or two. Take him away!" He snapped and the guards marched him out of the throne room, leaving Minos and Ariadne alone.

"Do you really intend putting him in the Labyrinth?" she asked.

"If they don't send the children, yes."

"It would be such a waste of a brave and handsome young man."

"That's the way it goes!" he shrugged.

"But you said yourself you know how hard it is to lose a son - why cause the same anguish to someone else?"

"Precisely because I have felt it!" he was getting irritated by her questioning.

"But two wrongs don't make a right!" she continued. "Making someone else suffer the way you have won't lessen your pain in any way!"

"Actually my dear, you're wrong there," the shark smile reappeared on his face. "It just might!"

"It won't! You're not being reasonable!"

"I think I am - and anyway, I'm the King! I don't have to be reasonable if I don't want to be!" He patted her cheek. "I can do what I like - that's the whole point of being King!"

"You can be so stubborn sometimes!"

"I don't see why you're so interested in all this," he said. "But since you are, you might as well make yourself useful - you can take his meals to him every day, I don't see why my servants should waste any time on the wretch."

"What? I'm a Princess! I don't do servants' work!" she scowled.

"You do in this case!"

"Why should I?" she folded her arms and almost stamped her feet but realised just in time that would make her look too much like a spoilt Princess.

"Look upon it as punishment for calling me stubborn," he wagged his finger at her. "Good daughters don't say things like that about their fathers!" And with that he swept out of the room again, leaving Ariadne alone with her thoughts.

Which were entirely to do with Theseus. The moment she set eyes on Theseus she thought there was something special about him. It wasn't just that he was handsome, she'd met plenty of handsome young men, it was something more important than just good looks. She liked the way he'd quietly stood up to her father, and the way he bravely accepted the thought of being sent into the Labyrinth.

It wasn't exactly love at first sight, but being given the job of taking his meals to him meant that she would get the chance to see him and talk to him three times a day and that wouldn't be a bad thing - at least she'd get to know him better.

After a couple of days, however, she began to have a horrible, growing suspicion that he wasn't particularly interested. He seemed preoccupied, as if he'd hardly noticed her. She lay awake at night, wondering what was going on. Of course he would be preoccupied, she thought to herself; he's in prison and may well be about to face a horrible death.

But then again, she thought, hasn't he even realised how unusual it is for a prisoner to be attended by a Princess? She decided to try to make a special effort to get noticed, so the next morning she arrived at his cell door with a larger tray than usual.

"Good morning!" She greeted him breezily once the guard had let her in. He was lying on the wooden platform he had for a bed, staring up the ceiling.

"Morning," he replied quietly, but at least he'd acknowledged her presence. The previous morning he'd hardly even done that.

"I've brought you some breakfast." She smiled as she set it down on the table at the other end of the cell.

"Thank you." He didn't move.

"I've brought bread and honey and fruit."

"Thank you." He still hadn't moved, and she didn't think he'd even looked at her.

"And milk. I brought quite a lot of fruit because I didn't know if there was anything in particular you liked or disliked. And three types of bread for the same reason."

"Thank you."

"Do you have any preferences?" she asked. She knew she was in danger of starting to witter and that would be a mistake but she couldn't help herself.

"Sorry?"

"Any particular types of bread or fruit that you're especially fond of?"

"Not really." He was still staring at the ceiling.

"Or particularly don't like?"

"Nope."

"Oh. What about lunch?"

"Eh?"

"What would you like for lunch?"

"I don't particularly care, really."

"Lamb?"

"Yes, fine. Thank you."

She could tell he was getting a little impatient with her. "Or fish?"

"I don't mind, really."

By now she knew she was wittering but she really couldn't stop herself. "Well which?"

"I don't mind. It's really not important to me!" he snapped.

"Oh," she was hurt by his tone, but tried not to show it. It might not have been important to him, but it was to her.

She started to cook the meals herself, taking great care over the ingredients and the cooking. And being able to say she cooked the meals herself gave her more chance to talk to him. And gradually he started to show a little more interest.

Well, in the food at least.

Which she took as showing a little more interest in her.

Which wasn't really the case. Which isn't to say he didn't like her, because actually he did. It was nice for him to have someone to talk to. Especially someone as pretty as she was, because frankly the guards weren't up to much.

But that was as far as it went. For him at least. He liked her, but he was a friendly person who liked most people. There wasn't really anything more to it than that. He didn't really think of her in the same way she was thinking about him. He had too many other things on his mind. But she didn't realise that. She thought he was starting to really like her, and that, in turn, made her like him all the more.

All this happened, of course, in the two weeks Minos had said Theseus should be imprisoned while they waited to see if the boat load of children arrived from Athens. Which of course it didn't. So after two weeks Minos chose the day Theseus was to be sent down into the Labyrinth. When he mentioned it to Ariadne she was horrified.

"Tomorrow? Why tomorrow?" she asked.

"Why not?"

"Well it's just that, er..."

"You're getting fond of that young man, aren't you?"

"No!" she tried to hide her embarrassment. "I just don't think it's right to feed human beings to that creature."

"You've never objected before."

"I suppose I've never really thought about it before."

"Then take my advice - don't think. Life's a lot easier and more pleasant if you leave the thinking to others. Now, are you going to tell him the news, or shall I?"

Ariadne didn't think she wanted to be the one to have to tell Theseus he was going into the Labyrinth the next day. She was about to tell her dad that he could do it when she suddenly had an idea. "It's okay," she smiled at her father, "I'll tell him."

At lunchtime she was let into his cell carrying a tray covered with a cloth. She waited until the guard had left before she said anything. "I've brought your lunch."

"Thanks," he smiled.

"And some news. You're going into the Labyrinth tomorrow."

"Good."

"Good?" she asked.

"That's why I'm here. I'll kill the monster and have all this over and done with."

"And have you thought about what you'll do after that?" she asked.

"How do you mean?"

"Even if you do kill the Minotaur have you given any thought as to how you'll get out of the Labyrinth? The whole point is it's impossible to get out once you're in. No-one ever has come out again. If you do kill the Minotaur you'll still be down there, probably for ever."

Theseus looked at her more closely than she thought he'd ever done and then said, "I must admit I hadn't thought that far ahead."

"No-one will be able to rescue you because to go into the Labyrinth would mean they would be lost in there as well."

"I hadn't thought of that, either," he admitted.

"It's just as well I have then, isn't it?" she said as she took away the cloth that was covering the tray to reveal a dagger and a ball of string.

"What's this?" he asked as she handed them to him.

"What does it look like? A dagger and a ball of string."

"And I'm supposed to fight a monster with it, am I?" She didn't like either the tone in his voice or the look on his face, but she ignored them both for the moment.

"Listen," she started to explain. "When they take you to the Labyrinth tomorrow the guards won't hang around, believe me. As soon as they've gone fasten one end of the string to something at the entrance and let the ball unroll as you go along the corridors. That way you'll be able to see where you've been and retrace your steps. If you do kill the Minotaur you'll be able to find your way out again."

"That's brilliant!" he was genuinely impressed.

"Thank you."

"You really are very clever," he said.

She held her hand up to make him listen. "If you find your way back to the point where you started there's another corridor to the right of the dungeons that leads down to the boat houses. From the boat houses there's another path that leads you up onto the cliffs and around to the harbour. Your ship is still waiting for you in the harbour. There won't be any guards around because they don't like being near the entrance to the Labyrinth and they don't see the need - nobody else has ever escaped. You should be able to get back to your ship without any difficulty, but be careful anyway."

"You really have thought this through, haven't you?" he said.

"Yes."

"I'm impressed."

"So you said. Thank you."

"No, thank you," said Theseus. "You've been wonderfully kind to me and I haven't always shown my appreciation, I know."

"That's all right."

"And what you've just done is incredibly brave. If I get away and your father finds out he'll realise someone must have helped me."

"I know."

"It won't be safe for you here any more. Come with me."

"What?" she couldn't believe what she'd just heard and needed to hear it again.

"Come with me," he said.

"Where?"

"To Athens. If your father finds out you helped me you'll be in real trouble. You have to come with me."

She wanted to be sure. "Do you want me to come with you?"

"Yes."

"No, I mean do you really want me to come?"

"Yes!" he said. "Meet me at the harbour. But be quick because we need to get away. We'll wait for you until dark."

"I'll be there!" her eyes had widened and there was a huge smile on her face. She kissed him and then turned round and left.

As soon as Ariadne kissed him Theseus knew he'd made a mistake. As he watched her rush out of the cell he realised that she thought he had asked her to come with him because he wanted them to be together. But it wasn't that. If her father knew what she'd done her life would be in danger and he couldn't see what else he could do but take her with him.

But he wasn't asking her to marry him or anything. He was just trying to do the honourable thing, be the gentleman he was brought up to be, but it had gone wrong.

He knew straight away he should have called her back and explained; but by the time he realised what she'd thought she was already out in the corridor. Besides, he didn't know how to explain without upsetting her and he didn't want to upset her. There was also, somewhere at the back of his mind, the slight suspicion that if he turned round now and told her she'd misunderstood she might not help him and he needed her help.

He knew that not telling her immediately that she'd misunderstood his intentions was the most cowardly thing he'd ever done in his life and he was ashamed. He tried to ease his conscience by telling himself that he had to clear this mess up when she brought him his supper, but deep down he knew he wouldn't, and he didn't.

He lay awake most of the night worrying what to do, and by sunrise he was determined to tell her when she brought breakfast. But it wasn't Ariadne who woke him up the next morning, it was two of the guards.

"Right then, Theseus, rise and shine! Come on!" one of them said as the other pulled his blanket away.

"What's happening?" he asked.

"You'll find out soon enough," the guard said cheerily.

"I haven't had my breakfast yet," Theseus protested.

"Ah well," the guard smiled, "that's because things are a little different today: you don't get breakfast this morning - you are breakfast!" The other guard seemed to find this rather amusing and they were still chuckling as they bundled him out of his cell and along the cold grey stone corridors.

There was such a deathly silence as they walked that even though he was barefoot it seemed to Theseus that his footsteps echoed along the corridors.

Suddenly the guards stopped. "Here we are," one of them said.

"This is it," said the other.

"Just go down these steps and follow the corridor as it bends to the right."

He tied one end of the ball of string to the frame and
then started to follow the corridor into the Labyrinth

"You're not coming with me?" Theseus asked. They laughed.

"No, mate! You are very much on your own from this point."

"But we'll stay here for a while," the other one said, "just to make sure you've gone in."

"So don't try any clever stuff like hiding round the corner "til you think we've gone and then coming out again."

"We'll be here for a while."

"Bye, then!" they laughed and pushed him towards the stairs.

They were so sure the Minotaur would kill him they didn't even check to see if he was taking anything in with him. Once he'd gone down a corridor and turned a corner he found a flaming torch mounted in a metal frame on the wall. He tied one end of the ball of string to the frame and then started to follow the corridor into the Labyrinth.

It got very dark very quickly.

He would have liked to have taken the torch with him, but he needed one hand to carry the ball of string and the other to carry the dagger. His eyes took a minute or two to adjust to what little light there was.

It took longer to get used to the smell. Rotting meat, discarded bones and animal waste littered the corridors. He had to be very careful where he trod.

He was horribly aware of the sound of his footsteps echoing along the corridors, even though he was treading as lightly as he could.

At the end of that corridor he found a dead end. Solid stone blocked his path. He followed the string back along the corridor and took another turning.

All the time he was treading lightly, breathing quietly, listening carefully for the Minotaur.

One dead end lead was followed by another and then another. He began to realise it was true - no-one could possibly have found their way out of this place. He silently thanked Ariadne for the string. Like all great ideas it was brilliantly simple, and simply brilliant.

Then he heard a sound. He stopped dead still and listened carefully, hardly daring to breathe. Then he heard it again. A snuffling sound, like that of a creature waking up. And not far away. But in the silence and the dark it was difficult to tell how far away.

Or how close.

He kept perfectly still and perfectly quiet. Surprise is a very useful tool in a battle. Until the Minotaur knew he was in the Labyrinth Theseus had the advantage over it. He knew the Minotaur's sense of smell was probably more highly developed than his own, but he hoped that the smell of the other bodies and the animal waste would disguise his own smell and give him a little more time.

He heard the sound again. To his left. He followed the string back to the turning he'd just taken and then turned left. But those few quiet footsteps were enough to alert the Minotaur and as Theseus entered a part of the Labyrinth where several corridors met, he met the monster. About thirty feet away at the other end of a corridor it stood sniffing the air. And then it lowered its head and looked towards him.

Theseus suddenly wondered if this was such a good idea. It wasn't that the thing was big - it actually wasn't as big as he'd expected. But it looked solid, like a huge heavy rock that couldn't be moved and yet could move very quickly and simply crush him to death. And then there was the smell. Of the monster and the air around it. The creature smelt of death itself.

He had to be very careful where he trod

Theseus took a step forward and stood on something that crunched under his feet. He looked down. When he saw what he'd stood on he couldn't help wondering, for a split second, who or what it had once been part of. And if one day someone else would accidentally stand on his bones as they faced this creature.

Just then he heard a voice inside his head saying, "Don't give in! Fight it!" It was partly his father's voice, partly Ariadne's, and he realised he had to fight; he had no choice. He couldn't let this thing frighten him. He stood up straight and proud and held his arms apart as if to make himself look bigger to the monster.

The Minotaur sniffed again and then lowered its head slightly. Theseus suddenly realised it was running towards him. It hadn't made any movement that suggested it was going to run, it just suddenly seemed to be moving very quickly towards him, almost as if some unseen force had hurled it along the corridor. What surprised him most was that the creature had lowered itself completely and was running towards him on all fours.

Theseus stood absolutely still until the creature had almost reached him and then slammed himself against the wall to take up as little space as he could and at the same time held his dagger out behind his back with one hand. The creature stormed past, still set on its course and unable, as Theseus had guessed, to react as quickly to the change in his position. As the creature passed him he caught it on the side with his dagger and it yelped.

Enraged and irritated more than hurt, it stopped and turned back towards its prey, but as it did so Theseus spun round and in one movement swiped the dagger across the Minotaur's chest and then ran quickly back down the corridor.

This time the creature was hurt, and now it was angry. It stood still for a moment as if to get its breath and then lowered its head, scraping its feet on the floor as if to get a firm footing. Then it lowered itself down to the ground and charged straight towards Theseus with alarming speed for an injured animal. Again Theseus stood still as it thundered towards him. At the last second he dropped down like a stone and rolled forward underneath it, striking the creature's stomach with his dagger as he did so. The creature turned quickly this time and, as Theseus came out from underneath it, caught him in the side with his horns, knocking him over and onto the ground. The creature's hooves seemed suddenly to rise in the air and then slam down on the ground just as Theseus moved over. One of the hooves caught him on the side of his ribs and for a second he was engulfed in pain as he felt two or three of his ribs being broken.

Out of the corner of his eye he saw the monster rearing up again and he knew this would be the end if he didn't move quickly. Despite the pain he rolled away quickly over the hard ground of the corridor and stood as best he could facing the monster. As it ran towards him he somehow found the strength to leap up, hold onto its shoulders and twist round through the air. Before it realised what was happening he was on the Minotaur's back, holding on for dear life with one arm as he stabbed his dagger into the creature's back again and again and again.

The sound of the creature's screams echoed along the corridor and filled the air to an almost deafening degree. Blood splattered over Theseus's face and arms and legs but this made him feel better because he knew that now he had to be causing the monster real pain. He stabbed the dagger into the creature's back again and again and again, feeling bone crunch and muscle collapse. Nothing could lose that much blood and survive for long, he knew, but it wasn't over yet. The creature fell onto its side and as Theseus fell off its back the Minotaur kicked him hard in the stomach; so hard it hurt, sending him flying through the air into the wall.

Winded and in pain, he knew he was a sitting target. He turned round just in time to see the Minotaur heaving itself up for one last attack but this time he was ready for it. The Minotaur was slower, more lumbering than before, and as it lurched towards him with the last of its failing strength, Theseus stuck his dagger into the creature's ribs and then in a swift movement pulled upwards to open the creature up before rolling over and out of the way.

The Minotaur fell to the floor breathing heavily. Breathing its last. One more blow to the neck and the creature was still, then silent. All that could be heard was Theseus's panting as he tried to get his breath back. He needed to take in as much air as he could, but every breath he took hurt his broken ribs even more.

And then there was another problem: he no longer had the string. They had fought at a place where several corridors had met and during the fight Theseus had become disorientated. He couldn't remember which corridor he'd come from or where he'd dropped the string. He couldn't even remember dropping the string.

Once he'd more or less got his breath back, he slowly retraced his steps to the junction of the corridors. He stood quietly at the junction, trying to let his mind relax. He knew he wouldn't find it if he thought about it; it was as if he knew he had to clear his mind and let the string find him. Slowly he sat down and carefully looked around him. His eyes were adjusted to the dark by now and he found he

One more blow to the neck and
the creature was still, then silent

could see quite clearly. Clearly enough, in fact, to begin to notice the differences between the corridors. He began to notice the different degrees of smoothness in the stones, the different textures, the different shades of dull earth grey; and gradually he began to recognise and remember the stones he'd walked past and the stones he'd slammed into. It took him a while, but he began to remember which corridors he'd walked along and where he'd come from. Within a minute of retracing his steps he came across the length of string, lying there as if it had been waiting for him all this time.

He traced his route back out of the Labyrinth and, as Ariadne had predicted, there was no-one there. There didn't seem any point in guarding the Labyrinth, no-one had ever got out of it. Until now.

He found the corridor which led to the boathouses and from there he found his way to the harbour. The path was rocky and slippery and every breath hurt his ribs and every movement reminded him that his whole body was in pain.

When he reached his ship his crew could not believe their eyes.

"How did you get out?" The Captain asked as he helped Theseus on board.

"It's a long story."

"You look terrible!"

"Thanks! I feel it too."

"Go and lie down. We'll get your wounds seen to as best we can but first we need to set sail right away."

"No! Wait! Is Ariadne here?"

"Who?"

"Ariadne. Minos's daughter."

"No," the Captain shrugged. "Why should she be?"

"It was she who told me how to get out of the Labyrinth.

I said we'd wait for her," Theseus explained. The Captain said nothing but the look on his face told Theseus what he was thinking. "She can't stay on Crete," Theseus explained, "If her father finds out what she did for me he'll kill her. She has to come with us."

"But we can't wait," the Captain argued. "If her father finds out you've got away he'll kill us all."

"I said we'd wait until dark for her, and that's what we'll do."

"Aye aye, sir," the Captain sighed and went to speak to the rest of the crew.

"Are we off, then?" one of them asked.

"No," the Captain grunted.

"Eh?"

"We have to wait until dark."

"What for?"

"Don't ask."

They took Theseus below decks and attended to his wounds as best they could while they waited in the harbour. His ribs were bandaged tightly and the cuts, gashes and bruises he'd suffered were bathed and covered with ointments. While this was being done the crew waited nervously, anxious to get away.

The Captain came down below to speak to Theseus. "It's dark now, sir."

"I know."

"With respect, sir, I think it's dangerous to stay here any longer. We need to get away."

"I know. Give it ten minutes."

"But sir -" There was a shout from up above to the Captain. The lookout had spotted someone running towards the ship. As the Captain came back up on deck the lookout shouted, "Who goes there?"

Out of the darkness came the reply "Ariadne, daughter of Minos."

"What are you doing here?"

"It's all right," the Captain said to his lookout, "I'll deal with this. Welcome aboard, Miss. I'll tell The Prince you're here." She ran along the gangplank onto the ship.

"He's here?" she asked. "How is he?"

"In a bad way, but he'll live if the Gods want him to."

"Take me to him. I'll tend him while you get this ship away. Set sail as quickly as you can. We don't have much time!"

"Yes, Miss," he sighed. "I am well aware of that."

When Ariadne went below and saw Theseus bandaged her heart went out to him. "Oh, Theseus! Brave Theseus!" she said as she knelt beside him and hugged him.

"Ouch!" he yelped in pain.

"Oh, sorry!"

"I think I broke a few ribs."

"Don't worry, I'll take care of you from now on. You just rest, I'll look after everything. The crew are getting ready, we should be off and away soon. Away to a new life."

"I want to thank you for everything you did."

"There's no need."

"Yes there is," he said, "it was a brilliant idea and I'd never have been able to get out again if you hadn't suggested it. You saved my life."

"And you saved mine," she said softly as she wiped his forehead with a damp cloth.

"How so?"

"By taking me away from my evil, horrible father. I've always known how wicked he was but I never dreamed I'd be able to escape to a new life. Especially not a new life with someone like you."

"Er," he cleared his throat. "I've been meaning to talk to you about that," he began, but she interrupted him.

"There's lots to talk about, I know," she smiled. "Lots of plans to make." Her voice was cheery and excited. "But first you need to rest. We'll have all the time we need to talk when you're better, but getting you better is the most important thing at the moment."

Again he gave up. Was it cowardice? Was he afraid of how she might react when he did tell her? Or was it just that he couldn't find the right words? He didn't know for sure, but what he did know was that he'd missed another chance and that with each missed opportunity the act of telling her the truth would become harder and harder.

The ship lurched slightly as the anchor was raised and it started to move away from its mooring. "There!" Ariadne smiled again. "We're away! Everything will be fine now, I promise. Just rest, I'll be here to look after you."

And that, in a way, was the problem. She was there by his side constantly. Looking after him, bringing him food and drink, tending his wounds. For the next couple of days she hardly ever left his side, and the more she did for him the harder he found it to talk to her honestly. The more he allowed her to do for him the more at home and happy she felt. Eventually he gave up trying and gave in to her wishes.

The poor girl had no idea what was going on. She thought she'd found a new life with the man she loved, the man she thought loved her. For the whole journey, all the time he was awake, she would talk about the things they would do together; the places they would visit, the home they would have; the fun they would have; the love they would share; the life they would share.

And in reply he said almost nothing. Hardly a word. The odd grunt and nod, because he didn't know what else to say or what to do to get out of the mess he knew he was in. He knew she was sweet and kind, good and pretty, and would make someone a wonderful wife, but not him. He didn't want to hurt her, but he didn't know how to go about telling her how he really felt without hurting her. So he didn't tell her at all.

And all that time she had no idea. When she talked to him, and all he gave in reply was a nod or a grunt or silence, she just assumed it was because he was still recovering from his ordeal and his injuries. Gradually his thoughts turned from how to tell her to simply how to get rid of her. And then the Captain came to see him and gave him the chance he was looking for.

"Sir, we think we're far enough away from Crete for it to be safe to pull in to the next port we can find and stock up on some supplies." He said. "The nearest island is Naxos and I know we can get most of what we need there. Will that be all right?"

"How long will it take?" Theseus asked.

"Well, there's a couple of things we need that might take a day or so, and there are a few repairs we need to make to the ship - she got a bit knocked about on the way out of Crete as we left in such a hurry. Should be two days, call it three at the most."

"That's fine," he said, his mind already hatching a devious plot. He was hardly able to believe his luck. This was an opportunity he hadn't expected.

When Ariadne brought him his next meal, he told her they had to pull in at Naxos. He explained that the crew would need to be able to carry out repairs to various parts of the ship. "So I thought it would be better if we slept on land for a couple of nights to let them carry out the work without us getting in the way."

"What will we do?" she asked.

"Well it depends. We might find a house to stay in, if not there's a tent on board so we could sleep in that for a day or two."

"Oh how romantic!" she cried, "that would be lovely!"

So the ship went into port and the crew set up the tent further up a hill overlooking the harbour. Theseus was strong enough by now to walk up the hill on his own, although Ariadne still insisted on helping. The crew brought up a couple of days' supplies for them before returning to the ship to carry out the work.

That night they had their first supper alone together, which Ariadne cooked over an open fire in front of the tent. When he finished Theseus lay back on the ground, looked up at the stars and sighed contentedly.

"How was the fish?" she asked.

"Wonderful, thank you. How was the wine?"

"Good," she smiled. "Very rich. A bit stronger than I'm used to, perhaps, but very good all the same."

"Have some more," he leaned over to fill her goblet.

"Oh, I don't know that I should! I'll be drunk!"

"No you won't! It'll just help you sleep well. That might be useful - it could be cold later."

"I suppose so. Oh, go on then! Cheers! Here's to us!"

He topped up both goblets, giving her just a drop more than him, and they clinked them together. Then he gulped all his wine down in one go.

"Ha! I can do that as well," she declared and downed hers in one go. Then she said "Oooh! Perhaps I shouldn't have done that. I feel a bit woozy all of a sudden."

"Go in and sleep," he nodded towards the tent. "You've worked hard, you need a rest."

"Mmmnn, I think you might be right," she said as she

got up. Once she was up she bent down again to kiss him. "Goodnight, brave Theseus!" she said.

"Goodnight kind, sweet Ariadne," he said, and he meant it. She was kind and sweet, but she wasn't the one for him. He knew what he was about to do was bad. He knew it was cowardly. But he told himself this was the first really cowardly thing he'd ever done in his life and he hoped that because it was the first the Gods would forgive him. He waited for a couple of minutes until he was sure she was asleep. He popped his head into the tent and could hear her breathing softly.

He turned and ran as fast as he could manage down the hill to the ship. Every step hurt. Each time he put his foot on the ground a pain shot up through his leg and into his back. His breath was short because he was trying to contain the pain. As he got further down the hill he could just make out his ship in the darkness. It seemed an eternity before he finally reached the ship. The crew were surprised to see him to say the least.

"Set sail as quickly as you can," he ordered the Captain.

"But where's the Princess Ariadne?" the Captain asked.

"She's not coming. Quick! There's no time to lose."

"Is everything all right sir?"

"It will be as soon as we're away. Let's go!"

"Aye aye, sir."

The sails were hoisted, the anchor pulled on board and they were off and far, far away by the time morning came.

And in the morning, in the tent on the hillside, Ariadne woke up feeling unwell and confused. She had a thick head, a dry throat, and felt a little queasy.

"Ugh," she grunted. "Uuuurrgh! I don't feel well. I told

you not to make me drink too much!" She looked around and realised she was alone in the tent. "Theseus?" she called, and when she got no reply she crawled out of the tent. "Theseus?" she called again. "Where are you?"

She looked all around her. She could see the sun, still low in the sky, slowly rising in the distance. A lone bird flew over some sheep that were quietly grazing. There seemed to be not a sound from anywhere. She gazed down the hill towards the port and she knew at the back of her mind that something was wrong with what she could see, but it took a moment for her to realise what it was. All the boats that had been there yesterday were still there. Apart from one. Theseus' ship wasn't there. She wondered at first why they'd had to move to a different mooring in the night but then as she looked more carefully at all the boats in port she realised it hadn't moved moorings. It simply was not there.

And neither was Theseus. Slowly, gradually, she realised what it all meant, but even when she'd pieced it all together she couldn't believe what had happened. He'd left her. Abandoned her. Alone on a hillside on an island she'd never been to before. After all that she had done for him. After all that was done and said between them.

And that was when she realised that actually nothing had been said between them. She had said it all and he had merely nodded or grunted or remained silent. Every time she'd told him she loved him his reply had been to kiss her on the forehead. He'd never actually said he loved her, and she'd been so wrapped up in her love for him she simply hadn't noticed. But now it all made sense.

She'd got it all so very, very wrong, and he'd never said a word. She'd saved his life, betrayed her father, abandoned her family and her home for him and at the first opportunity he'd abandoned her. She couldn't be with Theseus and she couldn't go home, and neither could she stay here. As she gradually realised the full extent of his betrayal, and all that it meant for her, confusion and sorrow were replaced by anger, which became furious outrage at what he had done.

She'd learned at an early age that breathing deeply helped to control emotions. She took a very deep breath and suddenly, from somewhere deep inside not just her body but her very soul, there erupted the most almighty, blood curdling, angry scream which shook the birds from the trees as it carried down the hill to the port. When it was finished there was absolute silence across the land and the sea. The birds flew away and didn't return. It was as if she was completely alone in the world.

She stood and looked out to sea. She couldn't see his ship but she knew it was there somewhere. She stood quite still and willed her thoughts to cross the air and the sea and to reach him. Why didn't you tell me? she thought. But she already knew the answer: because you lacked the courage! Oh, yes, you can take on a monster with your strength and a dagger but you daren't tell the truth to a girl! You pathetic wretch! You despicable little worm! How dare you treat me like that after I saved your life! It was me who saved you from the Minotaur, you wretch! Me! My brains! Not your strength, not your so - called courage! And this is how you repay me! Well we'll see who the brave ones are now! I have to face a life alone and with nowhere to go. I have to stay away from my family and my home and avoid my father for the rest of my life because I know he'll never forgive me for betraying him. I can cope with that, Theseus, I'll manage. But let's see how brave you and your crew really are. Let's see if you can face up to things as well as I can!

She took another deep breath and called out across the sea in a strong and booming voice. "I call on the Gods to

the most almighty, blood curdling, angry scream

avenge me!" she cried. "Poseidon, God of the ocean, hear me! Send a storm, I beg you, a storm to break his ship as truly as he has broken my heart!"

As her cry carried down the hill she could see the clouds beginning to move. It was almost as if the wind from her voice was pushing them together, and as they got closer together they grew dark and foreboding. When she finished speaking, her voice was completely lost. It was as if all the energy she had summoned into calling on the Gods had left her body and flown across the skies, taking on a life of its own. That force now gathered the clouds into a dark, heavy mass and pushed them away from the port, out to sea.

And once out at sea, it turned into an almighty storm.

Thunder and lightning, wind, rain and waves seemed to chase Theseus's ship, sending it one way and then the other. Masts cracked and woodwork fell. Everything that wasn't tied down rolled across the decks, knocking into the crew. Waves swept over the ship and threatened to wash the men overboard to a cold, watery death. They clung on for dear life. They fought the storm with all their skill and all their strength, fighting as one to keep the ship afloat as the sea seemed to throw everything it could at them.

And to their own amazement they survived. After the most terrifying and frantic two hours of their lives the storm seemed to quickly fade away, leaving the sea strangely calm and the sun high in the sky. Not one man had been lost overboard, and although the ship was damaged they found she was able to go on.

But more damage had been done than they realised.

It wasn't just Poseidon who heard her cries. Another God, Dionysus, happened to be nearby and when he heard her anguished cries he stopped to see who it was who was so angry and so heartbroken. He took one look at her and fell in love with her. So in love that he granted her wish, but in a way that would cause Theseus even more suffering than she had hoped for.

It was quite simple, really: when they sneaked away from Naxos they'd raised the white sails Aegeus had asked Theseus to use as a signal that he'd killed the Minotaur and was returning home victorious. But the white sails had been badly torn in the storm and were struggling to catch the wind. Theseus had fought the storm as bravely as his crew, but he was still weak and injured from his fight with the Minotaur and needed to rest. The Captain was worried that Theseus needed better treatment than they could give him on board, so to make up time he ordered the torn white sails to be replaced with the black ones.

With the black sails hoisted they travelled swiftly home while Theseus rested below deck, unaware that the sails had been changed over. The Captain was unaware of their significance.

All day every day since Theseus had set off for Crete, Aegeus had placed a watch high on the hills to look out for his return. They knew which ship to look out for, and which colour sails to hope for.

It was mid-day when the lookout recognised the ship sailing towards them. "Get the King!" he ordered one of the soldiers nearby. "Go get the King! It's Theseus's ship!"

"What about the sails?"

"I can't see - the sun's behind them. Go get the King anyway!"

The soldier scurried off, leaving the lookout squinting into the sunlight to see. "Oh, come on!" he thought aloud. "Move to port and then I'll be able to see you more clearly. I can't see a thing until you move!"

Elderly as he was, Aegeus ran swiftly to the lookout post. "Where is it?" he asked excitedly, "Where is it?"

"Over there, your royal highness," the lookout pointed to his left. "See it?"

"Ah, yes! That's it! My boy's on his way home!" the King was almost laughing with excitement. Then he turned to the lookout again. "You're certain it's him?" he asked.

"Yes, sir."

"And the sails? What about the sails?"

"To be honest, sir, at this distance I can't see for sure. The sun's too bright for me to be able to make out colours very clearly. We'll just have to wait until the ship's a little closer and the sun's a little higher. Shouldn't be long now. At this stage in the day the sun often seems to leap up suddenly higher into the sky. There! See? Suddenly everything's clearer now, isn't it, sir?" he looked at the King. "Sir?"

"Black," the King said.

"Sir?"

"They're black. The sails. Black. He promised to signal his victory by raising white sails. These are black."

"They may not be, sir," the lookout said. "It could still be the light."

"No. They're black, I can see quite clearly now," Aegeus said quietly. "He's dead. My son failed in his quest and he's dead. And it's all my fault."

"No, Sir, it's not your fault," the lookout tried to reassure him. "We can't be sure. We have to wait until the ship's closer to be sure."

"No, I'm sure. I know it."

"We don't know it yet, Sir, all is not lost."

"It is. All is lost if I've lost my boy, and I have. And it's my fault. There is nothing left to live for."

"Now don't start talking like that, Sir!" The lookout was feeling awkward and embarrassed. He didn't know what to say to the King.

"Why not?" asked the King, "It's true. There is nothing left to live for. So there's no point in my living any longer." And with that he jumped off the cliff.

It happened so quickly neither the lookout nor the soldier could do anything. Instinctively the lookout cried "No!!!" but all he and the soldier could do was watch as the old man's body fell down the cliff towards the coast and smashed on the jagged rocks below.

They stood still where they were, sickened by what they'd seen, unable to move. As the ship sailed closer they gradually realised they could see Theseus standing proudly on the bow of the ship waiting to greet his father. Without speaking a word to each other the two of them climbed down the path that led to the port to greet the Prince.

As the ship pulled in as close as it could to the harbour wall the lookout called out "Welcome home, your Royal Highness."

Theseus smiled at him graciously. "Actually that's the greeting you give to a King, not a Prince," he said, "but thank you anyway. Where is my father?"

There was an awkward pause. Neither the lookout not the soldier could find the right words. After a moment the lookout said, "As I said, Sir, greetings your Royal Highness. Theseus, King of Athens," he emphasised the word King, "we welcome your safe return."

"I don't understand," Theseus was walking along the gangplank towards them by now. "What's happened to my father?" They both knelt in front of him and the soldier tried to explain. "It was the sails, Sir. He saw the black sails and presumed the worst."

there's no point in my living any longer

And that was when Theseus understood. He hadn't even noticed the sails until then, and now, just as Ariadne had gradually put everything together as she stood looking down the hill towards the port on Naxos, he now realised everything on his return home.

His punishment from the Gods was to be made King. A very unhappy King. Even though he was loved by his people, and would be praised throughout the world for his courage and his slaying of the Minotaur, he knew from that moment on he was doomed to be never truly happy.

Even when he later married a woman called Hippolyte, who he loved dearly, and they had a son called Hippolytus whom he adored, he was still somehow not really, truly, completely happy. It was as if he was never at peace with himself because of what he'd done to Ariadne.

When, years later, Hippolyte died next to him in battle he somehow knew this was all part of the way his life was meant to be. The punishment would never end; one way or another it would continue for the rest of his life. He never forgot what he had done to Ariadne. It seemed as if he would never be never allowed to, and that he would never be forgiven.

Perhaps the Gods felt he still had a lesson to learn: there are different kinds of courage, and different ways of being brave. And just as there are different ways of being brave, there are different ways of being a coward.

Sometimes it takes real courage to treat people they way they ought to be treated.

In the mid 1970s, while I was a student in London, I worked in restaurants and hotels to earn extra money. One of these restaurants was 'Conrad's Bistro' in Belsize Park, and there I worked with a man called Nick who was originally from Greece. As we washed up, cleaned the kitchens and prepared the salads for the chefs Nick would tell me some of the old stories from Ancient Greece. This was the first time I'd heard these stories, and it was the beginning of my love for them.

I have no idea where Nick is now, but wherever he is I hope he's still telling the stories he grew up with. Just as Nick passed these stories on to me, I'm now passing them on to you. And I hope that you, in turn, will pass them on to someone else because that's how stories stay alive for as long as they do. And if you ever meet Nick, please thank him from me.

John Harris
Autumn 2006